SEAN STOCKDALE is a former Advanced Skills teacher for ICT and English, who is now Communications Manager for NASEN. This allows him to visit a range of education setting across the country, contribute to national special needs policy and see how teachers bring out the best in some of our most vulnerable young people. Sean is often asked to provide comment on special needs and inclusion issues for the national media, including the Independent and BBC Radio.

ALEXANDRA STRICK has worked in the children's book world for the past 15 years. At Booktrust, she managed programmes including Bookstart and Children's Book Week, was deputy executive director, and regularly reviewed children's books for the Guardian. She is now a consultant to Booktrust on all aspects of disability and diversity, as well as working with other agencies and charities (she is co-founder of Inclusive Minds, the collective for all those interested in diversity and books and also Outside In, the UK organisation dedicated to exploring books from around the world). She has delivered training for writers, illustrators and publishers on accessible and inclusive books, both in the UK and internationally.

ROS ASQUITH has been a Guardian cartoonist for 20 years, and has written and illustrated over 60 books for young people. Her books for Frances Lincoln include *The Great Big Book of Families* and *The Great Big Book of Feelings* with Mary Hoffman, and *It's Not Fairy*, which she wrote and illustrated herself.

For Emma, George and Oscar — S.S.
For Ella, Dan and all my family — A.S.
For Jessie, Lola and Lenny — R.A.

JANETTA OTTER-BARRY BOOKS

The authors, illustrator and publishers would like to thank Aminder and Tatinder Virdee
and all the children, families and professionals who contributed ideas and inspiration for this book.

Text copyright © Sean Stockdale and Alexandra Strick 2013
Illustrations copyright © Ros Asquith 2013
The rights of Alexandra Strick, Sean Stockdale and Ros Asquith to be identified as the authors
and illustrator of this work have been asserted by them in accordance with the Copyright,
Designs and Patents Act, 1988 (United Kingdom).
First published in Great Britain in 2013 and in the USA in 2014 by
Frances Lincoln Children's Books,
74-77 White Lion Street, London N1 9PF
www.franceslincoln.com

First paperback published in Great Britain in 2014

A CIP catalogue record for this book is available from the British Library.

ISBN 978-1-84780-519-5

Printed in China

3 5 7 9 8 6 4 2

MAX THE CHAMPION

Written by **Sean Stockdale and Alexandra Strick**

Illustrated by **Ros Asquith**

F

FRANCES LINCOLN
CHILDREN'S BOOKS

Max loved sport.
Night and day,
it filled his dreams!

When his alarm clock rattled, Max **jumped** out of bed.

He raced downstairs to breakfast.

At the breakfast table, Max **dived** into his cereal.

Then he buckled his helmet and **sped** off to school.

He **never** missed a turn.

At school, Max and his friends **flew** through their handwriting practice.

Max gave art his best shot, but somehow his picture was a bit **different**.

That afternoon, Max's school had **a fun** sports tournament with another school.

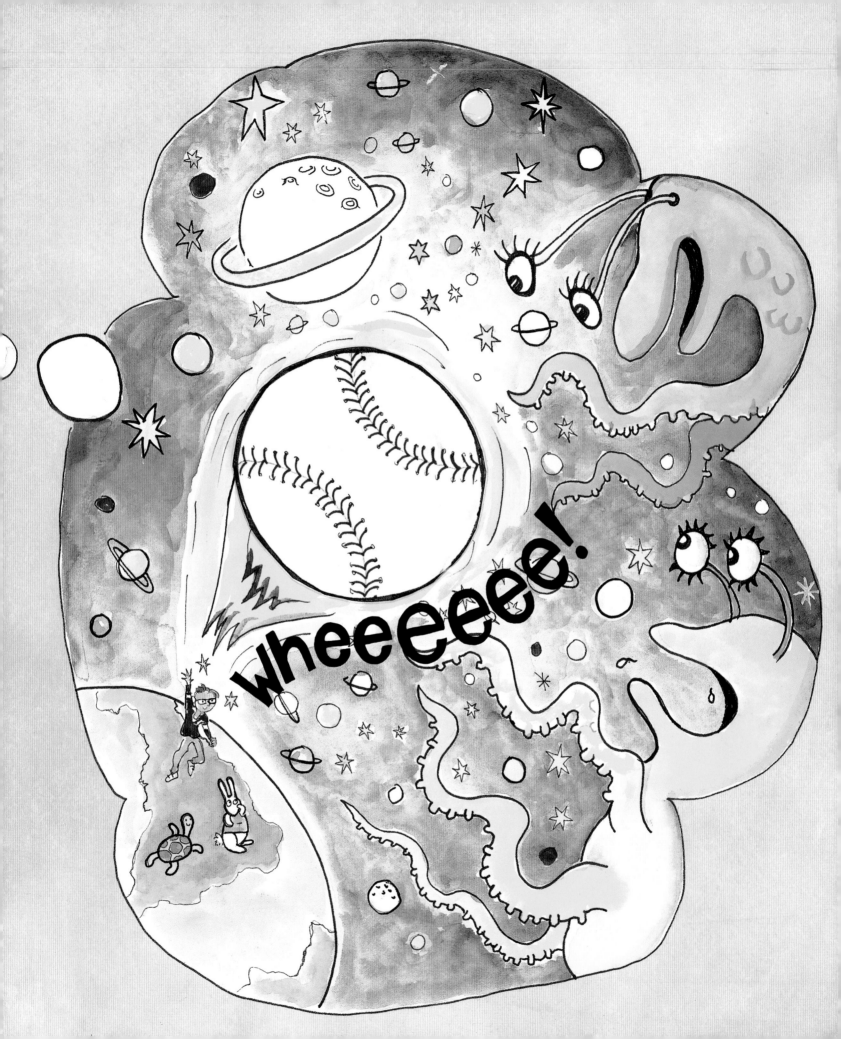

To celebrate winning the tournament, there was a special assembly at school. Everyone **cheered** as Max and his friends received their trophies.

The school bell rang
and it was time to go home.
Max **shot** out of the door...

and cycled home with his friends.

That night, as Max snuggled into bed,
a smile crept across his face.
Then he drifted happily off to sleep.
What a **dream** of a day.

Max, Booktrust and nasen

Sean and Alexandra's idea for *Max the Champion* came about through their work with Booktrust and nasen.

Booktrust is the national charity which aims to inspire everyone to enjoy books and reading. Nasen is the leading UK professional association embracing all special and additional educational needs and disabilities. Booktrust and nasen believe that we need stories and pictures which reflect all children – including children with additional needs.

Max is first and foremost a fun picture book about a boy with a powerful imagination. It also shows us that deaf and disabled children can – and should – be included, both in stories and in life.

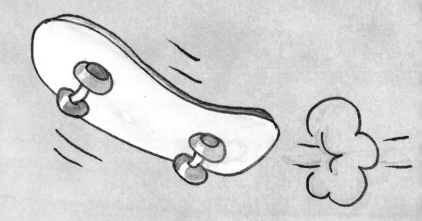

DISCOVER THE WONDERFUL *GREAT BIG BOOKS* SERIES, PUBLISHED BY FRANCES LINCOLN CHILDREN'S BOOKS

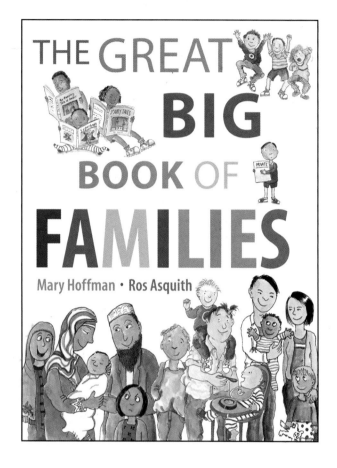

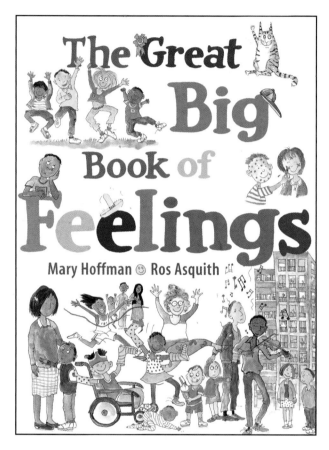

The Great Big Book of Families

Mary Hoffman and Ros Asquith

"Challenges preconceptions while reassuring children of all ages" – *Independent on Sunday*

Winner of the SLA Information Book Award

ISBN 978-1-84507-999-4

The Great Big Book of Feelings

Mary Hoffman and Ros Asquith

"A terrific book – essential for schools and perfect for families" – *The Bookseller*, Children's Booksellers' Choice

ISBN 978-1-84780-281-1

Frances Lincoln titles are available from all good bookshops.
You can also buy books and find out more about your favourite titles,
authors and illustrators on our website: www.franceslincoln.com